CHARLIE & MOUSE
EVEN BETTER

By **LAUREL SNYDER**   Illustrated by **EMILY HUGHES**

chronicle books · san francisco

For Mose and Lew. Always. And for Chris,
who does the grown-up jobs —L. S.

For Zach and Erin —E. H.

Library of Congress Cataloging-in-Publication Data:

Names: Snyder, Laurel, author. | Hughes, Emily (Illustrator), illustrator.
Title: Charlie & Mouse even better / by Laurel Snyder ;
illustrated by Emily Hughes.
Other titles: Charlie and Mouse even better
Description: San Francisco, California : Chronicle Books LLC, [2019] |
Summary: It is Mom's birthday, and Charlie and Mouse and their Dad want
everything to be perfect—so when the cake gets burnt the boys have to
come up with a new plan, pronto.
Identifiers: LCCN 2017045864 | ISBN 9781452170657 (alk. paper)
Subjects: LCSH: Brothers—Juvenile fiction. | Mothers—Juvenile fiction. |
Birthdays—Juvenile fiction. | Families—Juvenile fiction. | CYAC:
Brothers—Fiction. | Mothers—Fiction. | Birthdays—Fiction. |
Family life—Fiction.
Classification: LCC PZ7.S6851764 CI 2019 | DDC [E]—dc23 LC record
available at https://lccn.loc.gov/2017045864

Manufactured in China.

Design by Jennifer Tolo Pierce.
Typeset in Baskerville.
The illustrations in this book were rendered
by hand in graphite and with Photoshop.

10 9 8 7 6 5 4 3 2 1

Chronicle Books LLC
680 Second Street
San Francisco, California 94107

Chronicle Books—we see things differently.
Become part of our community at www.chroniclekids.com.

Contents

PANCAKES

Mom was making pancakes.

"These," said Mouse, "are the best pancakes ever."

"Yes," said Charlie. "But they could still be better."

"What would make them better?" asked Mom.

"They could be smaller," said Charlie.

"Smaller?" said Mom.

"They could be baby pancakes," said Mouse.

"Baby pancakes are special."

"You don't say," said Mom.

"Ta-dah!" said Mom.

"Babies!" said Mouse.

"Babies are the best," said Charlie.

"Mom is the best!" shouted Mouse.

"I wonder," said Charlie.

"What do you wonder?" asked Mom.

"I wonder if you could maybe make a turtle?"

"A pancake turtle!" said Mouse.

"I could try," said Mom. "I have never made a
pancake turtle."

"Ta-dah!" said Mom.

"Turtles!" said Mouse.

"Turtles are the best," said Charlie.

"Mom is the best!" shouted Mouse.

"I wonder," said Charlie.

"What do you wonder?" asked Mom.

"I wonder if you could maybe make a dragon?"

"A pancake dragon!" said Mouse.

"Hmmm," said Mom. "I have never made a

pancake dragon."

"Ta-dah!" said Mom.

"What is THAT!" said Mouse.

"A dragon," said Mom.

"It does not look like a dragon," said Charlie.

"No, it does not look like a dragon," said Mouse.

"It is a dragon," said Mom. "It is a dragon that annoyed its mother."

"How did it annoy its mother?" asked Charlie.

"It asked for too many pancakes," said Mom.

SHOPPING

Charlie and Mouse were going shopping.

Charlie and Mouse were going shopping with Dad.

It was a secret!

"Shhhhhh!" said Charlie.

"What do you think Mom might like for her birthday?" asked Dad. "Flowers? Bubble bath?"

"Yes," said Mouse. "Mom would like those. Mom likes smelly things. But they are not the things I want to buy."

"What do you want to buy?" asked Charlie.

"I am not sure yet," said Mouse. "Will you help

me think?"

"Of course!" said Charlie.

Charlie and Mouse thought. "Hmmm."

"Maybe Mom would like a jewel," said Charlie.

"Mom likes things that sparkle."

"That is true," said Mouse. "But we only have two dollars. I think a jewel will cost more than two dollars."

"Oh," said Charlie. "Then maybe Mom would like a special box to keep special secrets in. And we will promise not to peek in it, ever."

"Mom would like that," said Mouse. "But I am not sure I can make that promise. I like to snoop."

"That is a good point," said Charlie. "I like to snoop, too."

Suddenly, Mouse stood up. "I know!" he said.

"I know what Mom would like!"

"What?" asked Charlie.

"Tape!" said Mouse.

"Tape?" asked Charlie.

"Yes, tape," said Mouse.

"Does Mom like tape?" asked Dad.

"Everyone likes tape," said Mouse.

"That is true," said Charlie.

"Also, tape is a thing Mom can never find when she needs it."

"That is also true," said Charlie. "Tape is a very good idea. You are smart, Mouse."

"I try," said Mouse.

"Now you should wrap the present,"

said Dad, when they got home.

"I want to wrap the present," said Mouse.

"But I do not think I can."

"Why not?" asked Dad.

"I can't find the tape," said Mouse.

HELPING

Dad was baking a cake.

"Can we help?" asked Charlie.

"No," said Dad. "This is a grown-up job.

Why don't you make Mom a card instead?"

Charlie and Mouse made seven cards.

Dad was making special birthday chili.

"Can we help?" asked Mouse.

"No," said Dad. "This is a grown-up job. Why

don't you go outside and pick flowers instead?"

Charlie and Mouse picked *all* the flowers.

Dad was washing dishes.

"Do you want to help wash dishes?" asked Dad.

"No," said Charlie. "That is a grown-up job."

"Yes," said Mouse. "That is definitely a grown-up job. We will decorate instead."

"That is a fine idea," said Dad. "You do that."

Charlie and Mouse went to their room.

Charlie and Mouse gathered supplies.

Charlie and Mouse decorated.

"No, Mouse," said Charlie, "the snake goes

over here."

"Oops!" said Mouse.

"We have to be careful," said Charlie. "It needs

to be just right."

"I am always careful," said Mouse. "Careful is

my watchword."

"*Now* we are finished," said Charlie.

"Yes," said Mouse. "Now we are finished.

But it could still be better."

"What would make it better?" asked Charlie.

"If it was not so smoky," said Mouse.

SURPRISE

The cake was burnt.

The house was smoky.

"What will we do?" asked Mouse.

"Let me think," said Charlie.

"Think fast!" said Dad. "Mom will be home soon!"

Charlie thought fast.

"I have an idea!" said Charlie. "But Dad will have to help me turn on the stove."

"What is the idea?" asked Dad.

"No time to explain!" said Charlie. "Come on!"

"What about me?" asked Mouse. "What will *I* do?"

"You will distract Mom," said Charlie. "All by yourself. Can you do it?"

Mouse nodded. "I am up to the task!"

Charlie and Dad went away.

Mouse got ready.

Mom came home.

"Why, hello, Mom," said Mouse.

"Why, hello, Mouse," said Mom.

"How was *your* day?" asked Mouse.

"It was . . . nice," said Mom. "How was *your* day?"

"It was . . . eventful," said Mouse.

"Oh, my," said Mom. "You will have to tell me all about that."

"Later," said Mouse. "After you sit on the couch and hug me for four minutes."

"I am always happy to give you a hug,"

said Mom. "But why four minutes?"

"I have my reasons," said Mouse.

"Fair enough," said Mom.

Mom sat down.

Mom gave Mouse a hug.

Until the door swung open.

And in came Charlie with a plate!

"Ta-dah!" said Charlie.

"Ta-dah!" said Mouse and Dad.

"Wow!" said Mom. "What a surprise!"

"Surprises are the best," said Charlie.

"Mom is the best!" shouted Mouse.

"It's true," said Charlie. "Mom *is* the best."

"Yes," said Mouse. "But she could still be better."

"What would make her better?" asked Charlie.

"I do not know," said Mouse. "But she will think of something. She always does."